A Treasure Hunt for Mama and Me

Helping Children Cope with Parental Illness

by Renée Le Verrier and Samuel Frank, MD

Illustrated by Adam Taylor

NEW HORIZON PRESS
Far Hills, New Jersey

DEDICATION

To Pedro, for asking but never questioning — RLV

For my supportive wife, Jen — SF

New Horizon Press
P.O. Box 669
Far Hills, NJ 07931

Renée Le Verrier and Samuel Frank, MD
A Treasure Hunt for Mama and Me: Helping Children Cope with Parental Illness

Cover Design and Illustrations: Adam Taylor
Interior Design: Charley Nasta

Library of Congress Control Number: 2012945209
ISBN 13: 978-0-88282-436-9

SMALL HORIZONS
A Division of New Horizon Press

2017   2016   2015   2014   2013   1   2   3   4   5

Printed in the U.S.A.

Billy leapt from rock to rock, which made his pack thump against his back.

He splashed through puddles.

He scooped up a little green frog, studied it and then let the frog go.

"**M**ama?" he asked. "Did you bring the treasure bag?"

Tap, tap. She tapped her pack with the tip of her walking stick. "Yes, it is right in here."

Billy could hardly wait to add to the bag of magical treasures. The last time they walked through the woods he had collected a pinecone that was shaped like a mouse and two silver stones that glimmered in the sun.

Billy skipped along the wide path.

Soon Mama started to slip and stumble even though there were no tree roots or branches in the way.

"It is time for my medicine," she said. Mama shuffled to a wide ledge and sat down. "Now you can look for treasure," she said.

Zip, zip. Mama unzipped the small pocket on the side of her pack. Billy reached in until his fingers touched the soft cloth.

"I can feel the pinecone and the stones inside," Billy said. "There is room for more."

He pulled out the yellow bag with the drawstring top and set it beside Mama.

"Do other mamas need to take medicine?"

"Sometimes," Mama said. "My body is like a car that runs out of gas. The medicine helps me go again."

Billy's mama has *Parkinson's disease*. Her brain is losing its ability to send signals to the rest of her body that let her move smoothly. The disease also stiffens her muscles and can make her hands shaky.

"I liked the way we used to treasure hunt together," said Billy.

"Me, too," said Mama. "I will be right here. Now you get to surprise me with what you find."

Billy crouched low looking for something special.

A plump black spider crawled across a fern. Mama would not like a spider.

He stood up and spotted some sticks and twigs, but they were just plain brown sticks and twigs from a nearby oak tree.

He crept close to a hole in an old maple tree. It looked like a cave, so dark and—***oh!*** A flash of gold, white and brown and then out flew a bird bigger than Billy's whole head.

Billy ducked down to the leafy ground and squeezed his eyes shut.

When Billy eased one eye open, he spotted something soft and long with brown and white stripes on it.

Plucking it out of the air, he scrambled back to his mother who was still resting on the ledge. Billy showed it to her.

"What a handsome owl feather!" she said. "Owls are very smart—like you. What a special treasure."

Billy slid the feather into the bag with the pine cone and the stones and pulled the string tight.

"Would you like to carry the treasures?" Mama asked.

"Oh, yes," Billy said and, **zip**, he closed up the bag in his pack. "Are you feeling okay now, Mama?" he asked.

She nodded. "I am right behind you."

Billy climbed onto a tree stump, picked up a stick and waved it as though he were a king. After even more walking, he saw Mama's hands start to shake.

"Oh, my," Mama said. "It is time for me to rest again." Mama used her pack for a pillow.

She smiled her crooked smile. "Stay near," she told Billy.

Zip. Billy pulled out the yellow bag. As he set it beside Mama, he asked, "Do other mamas shiver when it's warm?"

"Sometimes," Mama said. "When my body feels like it has been driving on a really bumpy road, I need to pull over and rest for a while."

Billy wanted to find something extra special for Mama this time. He peeked under bushes, but he saw only dead leaves there.

He peered into a narrow split in a boulder. Nothing. Then he noticed how much wider the gap became at the top of the big rock.

"I wonder what is up there."

Billy started to climb. He felt the muscles in his legs working hard. Step after step, his toes gripped the rock as the path became steeper.

He could almost see over the top when ***step, scrape***, his boot slipped on a damp edge of stone. His other foot slipped too and down he slid.

Billy grabbed for a bulge in the rock but missed. All the way down to the bottom he slid. Scratches covered his hands and — ***oh!*** His right knee was bleeding.

He dashed back to Mama.

Before he could tell her what happened, Mama saw the blood. She took out a blue polka dot bandana and sprinkled it with water from her water bottle.

As she gently patted his hands and knees with the cool cloth, Billy felt the sting go away.

Mama hummed while she taped a bandage across the biggest scrape.

Billy didn't feel like humming. He had the owl feather, but he wanted to find more treasures.

Then he spotted something on the ground near the front of Mama's boot.

"Look, Mama!" He pointed to acorns joined at the tips of their caps. "Two together!"

"These are side by side," she said. "Like you and me. Now, that is special."

Billy slipped the acorns into the bag with the feather and the pinecone and the stones. He pulled the string tight. **Zip**, he closed his pack.

"Is your gas tank full now, Mama? Are you ready to drive again?" he asked.

She nodded. "I am right behind you."

Billy dragged a stick behind him making a long line through the pine needles. He stopped and listened to a woodpecker overhead digging for food. His stomach growled with hunger.

Mama stood behind him. "This is a good spot for lunch," she said. She reached into her pack and spread out a picnic.

After Billy finished his last oatmeal cookie, he played with the pinecone mouse and tickled his arm with the feather.

"It is time to start back," Mama said.

Billy tucked each treasure back into the bag and pulled the string. "I am right behind you," Billy said. He looped his arms through the straps of his pack.

Billy jumped between sunbeams. He marched with a stick baton.

At a muddy patch, he waited for Mama to slowly cross the log bridge over the stream before he hopped all the way across it on just one leg.

Mama leaned on her walking stick and smiled her crooked smile again. "Stay near," she said.

Billy swung his pack off his shoulders to reach for the yellow bag. The pocket was open.

"Oh no!" he cried out.

The treasure bag was gone.

He followed the trail back and searched through the leaves, under fallen branches and pieces of bark.

Nothing.

Billy kept looking. He balanced on the log bridge and—*oh!* There it was! The yellow cloth clung to a reed in the mud.

Billy grabbed a long stick and reached toward the reed. The stick did not quite reach the yellow bag.

Billy stepped down into the mud. One more step, reaching, reaching and he grabbed the bag but—*oh!*

He toppled into the mud.

"Mama!" Billy cried out. The mud felt like it was grabbing him and would not let go. "Mama!"

Mama already had her arms threaded under his. He hugged the treasures to his chest and felt her wrap him close to her and whisper in his ear, "I am right beside you."

Billy put on the dry socks that Mama had pulled from her pack.

Mama knelt beside Billy. "The treasures are special, because we enjoy them," she said. "The best treasure of all would not even fit in the treasure bag."

"What is it?" Billy asked.

"You!" Mama wrapped him up in a hug.

Billy felt her breath on his hair, soft as a feather. He looked up at Mama. Her eyes sparkled in the sun like the silver stones.

Ready?" he asked.

"I am right behind you," Mama said, standing close behind Billy.

Billy turned and grasped her hand, drawing her alongside him.

"Mama, we can be like the acorn treasure," Billy said. "We will walk side by side."

– The End –

Tips for Children

- Everyone's body works differently. Sometimes adults need to take medicine to help them feel better. Sometimes children do, too.

- It is okay to be near people with illnesses such as Parkinson's and Multiple Sclerosis , because they are not contagious. You cannot catch their illnesses the way you can catch a cold.

- Even though grown-ups in your family have to take medicine or get tired easily, they still love you.

- Sometimes it can feel scary when grown-ups are ill. Talk about your feelings with your family.

- When your mother or father is too tired or cannot listen and you want to talk, draw a picture or write your words down in a letter for later.

- Ask a parent to help you with ways to respond to questions that other children might ask.

- Your parents might not be able to do certain activities with you. That does not mean that they do not want to be with you. They do.

- Think of some ways that you can do an activity together that you all can enjoy.

Tips for Parents and Educators

The challenges that adults face when living with a chronic or degenerative condition can also impact the children in the family. Keep an open dialogue with your children and involve them in the adjustments to routines and modifications for working with limitations. These strategies can help replace your child's fear and anxiety with knowledge and understanding.

Talk

- There is currently no cure for many conditions such as Parkinson's disease, but treatments have advanced and adults can live active lives after being diagnosed with many illnesses. Reassure your child. Tell her you can still take care of her.

- Explain to your child that the condition is not contagious and that having the disease is also not Mom's, Dad's, a grandparent's—or the child's—fault.

- Disease symptoms, progression and need for help vary from person to person. Discuss your limitations as well as what you can do to help improve your symptoms, such as following certain diets and exercise plans.

Listen

- Allow children to ask and talk about the symptoms they have seen in their parents and how they feel about them.

- If it feels scary for your children to see an adult lose her balance or embarrassing to have a parent who is "different" from other parents, encourage them to tell a grown-up about it.

- Let children express how it affects them when:

  - you cannot do "regular" activities together such as play catch or go to a movie;

  - they may need to do extra chores;

  - one adult is caretaking for them as well as for another adult in the household.

Act

- Clarify that the parent's symptoms reflect the disease; they are not a reflection of the person. Walking slowly, for example, does not mean that Mom or Grandmother is slow intellectually.

- Talk about how your child could respond to comments from friends. Compare which situations may warrant no reply and how others could benefit from more information. For example, "No, my Dad isn't drunk. He has a condition. I can tell you more about it if you're interested."

- Advocate together. Investigate local chapters and organizations for family support groups or form a group at school. Consider joining awareness-raising events together in your area.

- Invite your children to share in diet and exercise programs with you. Consider cooking together. Dance, tai chi, yoga and walks can be a beneficial and fun way to spend time as a family.

- Talking, listening and remaining active with children who have adult family members with chronic illness can help relieve worry, uncertainty and unease.